To Dad, thanks for all our great Easter holidays!—SW

For Michelle Campanella, a hard-working,
year-round Easter Bunny.—CB

Scholastic Australia
345 Pacific Highway Lindfield NSW 2070
An imprint of Scholastic Australia Pty Limited
PO Box 579 Gosford NSW 2250
ABN 11 000 614 577
www.scholastic.com.au

Part of the Scholastic Group
Sydney • Auckland • New York • Toronto • London • Mexico City
• New Delhi • Hong Kong • Buenos Aires • Puerto Rico

Published by Scholastic Australia in 2019.
Words by Colin Buchanan © Universal Music Publishing Pty Ltd. 2019.
Illustrations copyright © Simon Williams, 2019.

 A catalogue record for this
book is available from the
National Library of Australia

NATIONAL
LIBRARY
OF AUSTRALIA

ISBN: 978 1 74299 256 3

Typeset in Supernett.

Printed in China by RR Donnelley.

Scholastic Australia's policy, in association with RR Donnelley, is to use papers that are renewable and made efficiently from wood grown in responsibly managed forests, so as to minimise its environmental footprint.

10 9 8 7 6 5 4 3 2 1   19 20 21 22 23 / 1

When the EASTER BUNNY went on HOLIDAY!

Colin Buchanan

Simon Williams

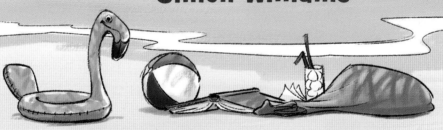

A Scholastic Australia Book

Once the Easter Bunny
   Told them all in Canberra,

'Give me a beach bag

I need a break!

'Cos Australia's enormous,
I'm **puffed**
and **pooped**
and **tuckered out!**'

So the Easter Bunny

Went on holiday.

We'll need an Easter **koala**,

An Easter **goanna**,

With the **wombat** and **kangaroo**
Help's on its way!

Tell the bilby and bogi,
'Cos they're true blue and dinky di,
The Easter Bunny went on holiday!

Well, the word spread **quickly**
On the old bush telegraph
From gum tree to **outback**
To old **billabong**.

All of the animals
Were keen as beans to lend a hand.
They all sang this
Aussie Easter song:

Easter **koala**,
Easter **goanna**,
Easter **wombat**,
Easter **kangaroo**!

Bilbies, bogis
All of us are dinky di!

This Aussie Easter will be true blue!

Well they **gave** out the eggs,
That mob of Aussie animals
Then they headed to Canberra
In one **big** line . . .

'I'll tell the Easter Bunny,'
Said the proud Prime Minister,
'You can help him again
Next Easter time!'

Easter **koala,**

Easter **goanna,**

Easter **wombat,**

Easter **kangaroo!**

Bilbies, bogis
All of them are dinky di!
This Aussie Easter has been true blue!

So that's how the animals
Delivered **all** the Easter eggs . . .

When the **Easter Bunny** went on **holiday**!